SHOPPING

Story by GUYON BROOKE

Pictures by NANCY MEYERHOFF

WONDER BOOKS • NEW YORK

A Division of GROSSET & DUNLAP, Inc.

S ALLY SNAPPIT was going shopping in the new super-market with her mother and her baby brother. Sally gave a hop and clapped her hands. "Is it big? Are lots of people there? May I buy something?"

"We'll see," her mother promised as they went through the big doors.

Sally saw string beans and lima beans, yellow beans and baked beans, apples and bananas and cheese. Lamb chops, pork chops, steaks and hams, jams and jellies and pies. Chickens to be fried and chickens to be stewed, and holiday turkeys to roast.

Big fish, little fish, thin fish, fat fish, shrimp and lobster
and crab. And rows and rows of food in cans. The supermarket was very big and Sally Snappit felt very small, but
she was glad she had come!

Mother put the baby in a seat on a cart. The baby laughed and kicked his heels. Mother picked up a bottle of milk. "Do they have cows here, too?" Sally asked.

"No, but cows give the milk and the supermarket gets it in cartons and in bottles. Would you like to carry a cow home?" Sally wouldn't. "Or a little red hen?" Mother asked, putting eggs beside the milk. "The supermarket brings these foods in from farms."

Sally stopped to look at a round yellow pumpkin in the fruit and vegetable section. "Look, Mommy, a jack-o'-lantern," she cried. "All it needs is a face!" "That's right," Mother agreed as she weighed some potatoes. "Do potatoes grow in the back yard here?" Sally asked. "No, they grow in the ground out in the country, and the supermarket brings them in here on trucks. Then people like you and me come along and buy them for our supper." They walked on down the aisle.

"Look," Sally squealed, "there's my favorite cereal." On the shelf before them were giant boxes of cereal and teeny boxes of cereal. Some had pictures of pirates or pixies on them. Sally's favorite cereal, she knew, had a picture of Red Riding Hood and the wolf on the box. While Sally reached for it, her mother picked up a loaf of bread and a package of sugar cookies.

"Where does cereal come from?" Sally wanted to know.
"From grain," her mother said. "It grows in big sunny fields.
Then, when it is harvested, it is made into different things,
like cereal and bread and sugar cookies."

Sally thought about this as she walked to the meat counter. She stared at the bacon and chops, the meat in packages, the steaks and her favorite hamburger meat. "This is an awfully big icebox," she said slowly. "It certainly is," her mother laughed. "Otherwise, we'd have to go all over the country to get this meat—to cattle ranches and pig farms and sheep farms."

"And look at all these fish," Sally cried. "They're all looking at me!" Her mother smiled.

"Fishermen caught those fish in different waters—in brooks and lakes and rivers and oceans." Sally closed her eyes tight. She could see the fish swimming in the sea and the fishermen fishing for the fish. "And can we pick out what we like best?" Sally asked. Her mother nodded yes and walked down the aisle.

Sally saw laundry soap and clothesline rope, polish for shoes and paper towels to use, things in bottles, things in boxes and things in little round cans. "We have some of these things at home," she told her mother, "but where did the supermarket get theirs?"

"From places called factories," Sally's mother told her. "Busy people make them there, and then they are delivered in big trucks. Next time Daddy takes us for a ride on the highway we'll watch for some of those trucks." Sally thought that it was a good idea.

Suddenly Sally sniffed. She smelled cinnamon and clove and all the spices she smelled when her mother baked at home. Next to the spices Sally saw large green and black olives, dates, nuts and figs. "These come from all over the world on boats," her mother told her, and they headed for the check-out counter.

Sally helped take the groceries out of the basket and put them on the counter. "Shall I charge for the baby?" the clerk asked with a twinkle. "Oh, no!" Sally said quickly. "We brought him in with us. But don't forget the book—I'm buying it with my very own money."

That night, as the family sat down to eat, Sally Snappit told her father all about her first trip to the supermarket. "That's where we bought your dinner, Daddy," Sally said.

Then Sally Snappit ate her hamburger and baked potato and drank all her milk. And, at bedtime, Daddy read to her from the book that Sally had bought at the supermarket with her very own money.